Shakespeare: stories for today

Sarah Curtius

Bibliografische Information der Deutschen
Nationalbibliothek:

Die Deutsche Nationalbibliothek verzeichnet diese Publikation in der
Deutschen Nationalbibliografie; detaillierte bibliografische Daten sind im
Internet über http://dnb.dnb.de abrufbar.

Herstellung und Verlag: BoD – Books on Demand,
Norderstedt

ISBN: 978-3-7568-3255-2

Contents

"Not for an age but for all time"

William Shakespeare was born in Stratford in 1564. By 1592, his plays were being performed in theatres in London. Shakespeare wrote and performed plays in the most popular acting company in London, the Lord Chamberlain's Men. In 1599 they built their own theatre, the Globe in Southwark on the south bank of the Thames. He and his actors performed for Queen Elizabeth I and King James I. He retired and moved back to Stratford in 1613 when the Globe burned down. He died in 1616, aged 52.

We have thirty-seven plays which are believed to have been written by Shakespeare. In 1623, two of his friends published his plays in a collection called the First Folio. In the preface to the plays, another writer, Ben Johnson wrote that Shakespeare was "not for an age but for all time".

More than 400 years after his death, Shakespeare's plays are still performed all over the world. People love the comedies and still find them funny. People admire the tragedies and their studies of human nature, for example, the corrupting nature of power in *Macbeth*. Shakespeare's history plays have forever changed how we think of historical persons like 'evil' *King Richard III* or 'good' *King Henry V*. His plays are performed in traditional costumes or re-imagined in a modern context.

The plays have also been adapted in different forms. Verdi wrote an opera based on *Othello*. There have been many ballets based on Shakespeare plays, including Prokofiev's *Romeo and Juliet*. In the 20th century, there have been popular musicals based on the plays, like *West Side Story* (*Romeo and Juliet*) and Kiss Me Kate (*The Taming of the Shrew*). Books have re-told Shakespeare's stories and the stories have even been re-told in children's films: *Gnomeo and Juliet* is a version of *Romeo and Juliet* with garden gnomes and a happy ending, while *The Lion King* is a version of *Hamlet* with singing animals in Africa!

This collection of stories is not a re-telling of the plays. Instead, it takes individual characters from three of Shakespeare's comedies and imagines their stories in a modern setting.

The first story has the craftsmen from *A Midsummer Night's Dream* preparing to do a performance for a wedding party. It is a funny story with some fantasy elements.

Then we re-imagine the story of Portia and Bassanio and their friends Nerissa and Graziano, just some of the characters from *The Merchant of Venice*. We think about how Portia and Bassanio might date in the 21st century and who the evil lenders are in today's world.

Finally, we place the main characters from *Twelfth Night* into our world. People are often surprised that Shakespeare's tragedies have amusing scenes and that his comedies can be quite dark and have some troubling plots. In Shakespeare's play, the twins Viola and Sebastian are washed up on the beach of a strange country after a shipwreck and have to be creative to survive in their new home. My version of this story has a darker background as it reflects the experience of migrants in the UK today.

Each story is introduced with a summary of the original play ("Shakespeare's original") and a short chapter about vocabulary or language ("Language focus"). The first "Language focus" looks at words we use to describe people and their reactions. These are words which you will read often in the stories.

The second one compares the process of finding a partner in the 16th century and the 21st and looks at some specific vocabulary used.

The final "Language focus" highlights some of the references from Shakespeare's original plays which are hidden in these stories.

I hope you enjoy the stories and maybe it will encourage you to find a version of the original plays. Shakespeare's stories truly are "for all time".

A MIDSUMMER
NIGHT'S DREAM

Shakespeare's original

Why is the play called "A Midsummer Night's Dream"?

Midsummer Night is the longest day of the year. It is also sometimes called summer solstice. As a pagan festival, people celebrated this night by lighting fires, dancing and drinking. They believed that fairies and evil spirits would visit them in the night. In Shakespeare's play, the fairies interact with the humans and play tricks on them.

What's the original play about?

The play has three groups of characters:

• the couples at court

• the craftsmen who are the actors in the play within the play

• the fairies

The characters from these separate worlds meet and mix in the play.

The play starts in the world of the court where the Duke of Athens, Theseus is preparing to marry the Queen of the Amazons, Hippolyta. The duke is asked to help a nobleman who wants his daughter Hermia to marry a man called Demetrius who is in love with her. However, Hermia is in love with Lysander. We also learn that Hermia's friend Helena is in love with Demetrius. Hermia and Lysander decide to run away together. Helena tells Demetrius about their plan. He decides to follow them and Helena follows him. So, all four lovers find themselves in the woods outside of Athens.

We then meet the group of craftsmen who want to perform a play for the duke's wedding. They arrange to meet and practice in the woods. The most dominant player in the group is Bottom who wants to play all the roles.

By coming into the woods, the humans have entered the space where a group of fairies live. They are ruled by Oberon and Titania who are arguing. Oberon asks his servant Puck to help him have his revenge on Titania by dripping the juice of a special flower into her eyes while she is asleep. When she wakes, she will fall in love with the first thing she sees.

After Puck has dropped the juice into Titania's eyes, he finds the craftsmen rehearsing in the woods. He makes Bottom look like a donkey and makes sure he is the first thing Titania sees when she wakes up.

He and Oberon also see the young lovers and Oberon tells Puck to help. However, he gets it wrong and both men end up in love with Helena.

By the morning, all the confusion is resolved. Oberon frees Titania from the spell and they are reconciled. Puck takes away Bottom's donkey head and he goes back to his friends. The young lovers are discovered by Theseus and Hippolyta who are out hunting. Hermia and Lysander are in love with each other again, and Helena and Demetrius are also now in love. The couples agree to marry that day with Theseus and Hippolyta.

At the wedding feast, Bottom and the craftsmen perform their play and the fairies come to bless the marriages.

What about this version of the story?

In this version of the story, I have focused on Bottom and the other craftsmen. Can you find the elements of the story which are similar to the original?

Language focus

Body language

The stories have a lot of vocabulary to describe people and how they act and react. We communicate not just by what we say, but *how* we say it or even what we do *not* say. Here are some of the words you will find in the stories.

Let's start with some words for <u>describing people</u>.

It would be very rude to call someone **fat**, so we usually use different words like round or to have a full figure. Informal words to describe someone who is a little round are **chubby**, tubby, chunky, **stocky**, or plump. If someone is chubby, their clothes may be a **snug fit**. That means they may be a little tight.

For the opposite of fat, we could say someone is **thin**. Slim is a positive word, while skinny is more negative. If someone is tall and thin, we might call them **lanky**.

If you are thinking about someone's mood, they could be happy or sad. They could be in a bad mood (**grumpy**) or they could be extremely angry about something (**furious**). If they are nervous, then they might behave in an **awkward** way which means that their behaviour is stiff or shy and shows that they do not feel relaxed or confident.

Clothes

A piece of clothing or a new haircut which looks good may be called **fetching**. Another word to describe something that looks good is **flattering**.

The opposite could be described as **tatty** or **scruffy** which means untidy or dirty.

Reactions

There are so many different human reactions. If you are surprised by a piece of news, you could say you are amazed or maybe **stunned**, if you don't know what to say. If you do not know what to say, you may **hesitate** or wait a moment before you speak. If you are very surprised or shocked, you might **gasp**, which means to breathe in sharply.

These are quiet reactions but if you are really angry about something you might shout or **yell**. If you are sad or upset, you might have tears in your eyes or even cry or **sob**. Another reaction would be a **groan**. If you groan, you make a long sound while breathing out, usually because you are unhappy or in pain, although it can also be because you have heard a terrible joke!

When people interact, they often smile or grin. A **grin** is a smile where you show your teeth. A nervous laugh is a **giggle**. We often use this word for the way children laugh. If you find something really funny you might **burst out laughing**. Smiling and laughing is usually friendly. The opposite is **frowning**. That is when your eyebrows move closer together and you have wrinkles in your forehead.

If you agree with something, in English-speaking countries, you move your head up and down. This is called **nodding**. If you disagree, you shake your head from side to side.

If someone does not know the answer to something or does not care, they move their shoulders up and down. This is called a **shrug**.

Our eyes express a lot of emotion. You might **wink** at someone. This is when you close one eye for a short moment. An unfriendly gesture is a **glare**. If you **glare** at someone, it shows you are angry or annoyed about something.

Another way to show you are annoyed is to **roll your eyes**. If you do not believe someone, you **raise your eyebrows**. One final thing we do with our eyes is **stare** at someone which is when we watch someone or something very intently for a long time. Children in the UK are always told it is rude to stare.

Eating and drinking

If you **wolf down** your food, you eat it very quickly.

There are lots of words for drinking very fast, like to gulp, to guzzle or to chug. For drinking slowly, we say **sip**.

Bottom - a star is born!

VOCABULARY

If someone is in the **limelight**, they are the centre of attention.

Nuptial is an adjective for things to do with a wedding.

A **badge** is a small object which may be fixed to your clothes with a pin. It often has a picture on it. If you are wearing a suit jacket you might put a badge on your **lapel** which is the part of the jacket which is turned back and attached to the collar.

Nick woke to find the sun shining through a gap in the curtains. He hadn't even opened his eyes and he was already in the limelight. He chuckled to himself. Tonight was the first meeting of the Amateur Theatre Excellent Nuptial Shows (AThENS). When Nick had auditioned, Pete, the Creative Director had been speechless. Because Nick was so good ... obviously. This was his chance to become a world-famous actor. He was sure of it. He could see his name in lights: NICK BOTTOM.

"You out of bed yet, Nick?" his mother called up the stairs. Back in the real world, Nick still worked in the local cotton mill. "Just getting up, mum," he called and rolled out of bed with a groan and walked to the bathroom.

As Nick walked to the bus stop some time later, he caught a glimpse of himself in the window of one of the shops. Maybe his mother was right – his hair was getting a little long and messy. But this was the look of a serious actor, he was sure of it. He could imagine himself being interviewed about his latest film, looking ... serious, intense, intelligent and sexy. Pushing his long hair behind his ear, he would talk about the challenges of playing tragic roles. The interviewer would congratulate him on how a slightly chubby man like himself was so effortlessly sexy ...

"Morning, Nick!" The voice shook him from his daydream. It was Frank. Frank worked in the mill, too. He fixed the machinery. He was a tall, lanky lad with a squeaky voice. He was friendly and chatty and Nick liked him. In addition, Frank was also a member of AThENS and it was important that actors like them supported each other.

The two chatted about the evening meeting all the way to work and agreed to go to the meeting together after their shift. The day in the mill was mostly boring, except for the glimpses of Jenny Titan when she left the office to do an errand for the boss. She was a real beauty. She was small and slight, almost like a fairy. At least in Nick's eyes, she was an angel. She smiled shyly at him when she passed him and he smiled back but he never had the courage to ask her out. She seemed to live in a different sphere. He didn't stand a chance.

Just after lunch Nick had a visit from Mr Starveling. His business card said: "Robin Starveling. Fashion Designer. But Nick knew that his small sewing workshop in one of the local villages sewed specialised clothes for cleaning staff. Robin Starveling was a short, stocky man with thick glasses which he kept pushing up his nose. He was going a little bald but tried to cover it by combing his hair over his bald spot. Whenever Nick saw him he was wearing a cravat. He obviously thought he was cool. Nick thought he was a nerd.

Mr Starveling had come in to pick up an order of hardwearing cotton and chatted to Nick as he usually did while he waited for the order to be brought from the storeroom. As they were talking, Nick noticed the badge on his lapel. It was of the two masks from Greek theatre. "Are you an actor, too, Mr Starveling?" Nick asked casually. "Yes, I am!" Starveling replied enthusiastically. "I have just joined a theatre group actually. It's our first meeting this evening." "You don't mean AThENS, do you?" Nick asked. "Yes. That's right!" "Then we'll be acting together, my friend," said Nick and gave a little bow. Starveling grinned from ear to ear. "So cool! Call me Robin. I look forward to seeing you later!" The rest of the afternoon flew by as Nick kept thinking how nice it was to feel part of the acting community. He didn't have much to do and his thoughts returned again and again to the mental image of a cinema with big posters and his name NICK BOTTOM all over them. This was his destiny. He knew it. Fame – here I come!

Bottom down the pub

8th June

VOCABULARY

The **plot** is the story of a play, book or film.

When someone dies, they may be buried in a hole in the ground called a grave or in a large stone structure called a **tomb**.

When it is cold, you might wear a **cloak** instead of a coat. It has no sleeves. It is what superheroes like Superman wear.

If you **assert yourself**, you behave in a confident way.

If you perform a play, you will probably need some objects to use on stage. We call these objects **props**. You will also need to practice with the other actors. This is a **rehearsal**.

If you are in a rush, you might tell people, **"I've got to dash!"**

The group were meeting in the pub so Nick and Frank decided to have a pub meal and a pint before the others arrived. Frank ordered a steak and kidney pie with mashed potatoes and extra chips, plus a sticky toffee pudding with custard for dessert. Nick was having fish and chips. With salad because he was on a diet. As he watched his friend wolf down his food, he wondered how Frank managed to eat so much and stay so skinny.

As Nick put the last chip into his mouth, Robin came into the pub, looking very excited and wearing an even more brightly coloured cravat than earlier. They were soon joined by Pete who had brought a friend from work called Snug. Snug was a tall, muscly young man. Pete and Snug worked on a building site. Snug was tanned from working outside and obviously kept himself in good shape. His t-shirt was quite a snug fit, Nick thought and tugged at his own shirt which was also sitting quite snugly around his stomach after that fish and chips. He sucked his stomach in and gave Pete and Snug his best Hollywood smile.

Finally, as Nick got another round of drinks, a middle-aged man with rounded shoulders arrived and slid up to Pete. "This is Tom," Pete said to the others. "Now we're complete!" "What?! No girls?" said Snug in a very disappointed tone. "No," said Pete, "I told you. We're a serious theatre group. Men only, like in Shakespeare's day". "Okay, okay," said Snug as the group moved from the bar to a small table in the corner of the pub. Tom helped Nick carry the drinks to the table. Nick noticed Tom had pocketed the change although Nick had paid. Nick decided not to say anything. "So, what do you do, Tom?" Nick asked, trying to make polite conversation. Tom shrugged, "Oh, you know. This and that." Nick didn't know but he nodded and smiled.

Pete cleared his throat and spoke to the group. "So, as you know, I founded this group to fill a gap in the market. Wedding bands and discos are so yesterday. Nobody really wants to dance around after a good meal at the wedding reception." True, Nick thought tapping his tummy, very true. "Wedding theatre groups – that's the future! People want their wedding day to be a really special occasion and what better way to do that, than to invite your friends and family to a theatrical performance after the wedding reception?" Pete expected a more enthusiastic reaction, but everyone was sipping their pints. He continued. "Anyway, after much thought, I have decided that the best idea for our first performance is a really classic story." "Like Romeo and Juliet?" Frank suggested. "Not very cheerful for a wedding. They're all dead at the end," Tom said. "Yeah, and we haven't got any girls!" said Snug and rolled his eyes.

"No," said Pete. "More classical than that. The tragic story of Pyramus and Thisbe!" As Pete looked around his group of actors most of them had their glasses suspended just in front of their mouths in disbelief. Only Robin nodded enthusiastically. "I always loved Ovid at school! So cool!" "Ovid – are you for real?" said Snug. "Who did you two go to school with? Boris Johnson?"

Pete looked disappointed. Pete was the Creative Director. He was the man deciding who played the roles. Nick knew he should say something quickly. "It's an … interesting concept," he offered and smiled encouragingly at Pete. "What's the plot?"

Pete looked relieved. "Well, it is a bit like Romeo and Juliet, actually. Two young lovers are stopped from meeting by their families. They talk through a hole in the wall and agree to meet at a tomb." "A graveyard? Very romantic", said Snug sarcastically. Pete ignored him and carried on, "Thisbe arrives at the tomb and sees a lion. She runs away but drops her cloak. When Pyramus turns up, he sees the lion with the cloak and thinks the lion has eaten Thisbe so he kills himself with his sword. Then Thisbe comes back, sees Pyramus dead and kills herself with his sword." Robin put his hand on his heart and sighed, "So tragic. So moving. So cool." Nick glanced at Snug to see his reaction but he was no longer paying attention. He was making eyes at two pretty girls sitting at the bar who were looking at him and giggling.

"So, who's who?" said Nick who was keen to get down to business. "Ummm. ..." mumbled Pete, starting to shuffle through his notes. "I hate to point out the obvious," said Tom, "but as Snug keeps reminding us: we don't have a girl." "We need to find creative solutions! We shouldn't be limited by our ... limitations" Robin said, getting so excited he knocked the table and everyone had to steady their glasses.

"Yeah, but who's going to play Thimble or whatever her name was?" asked Frank nervously. "I could do that," Nick suggested. His fellow actors looked him up and down and their faces said NO. Nick tried again. "Or I could play Pyramus." Robin was thoughtful. "Have you thought how we could do the lion?" "Ummm," started Pete again but before he could continue, Nick said a little too loudly, "I could play the lion!" The people at the other tables stopped talking and stared at the group. Frank laughed and said, "Nick, you'd scare them half to death!" "I'd do it gently," said Nick who was a little hurt that Frank had laughed at him. Pete asserted himself, "Nick, you can play Pyramus!" Nick looked delighted. The leading role. The hero! He had to text his mother! She'd be so proud. He reached for his phone and started texting.

"So, who will play the lion?" Robin asked. "Snug, what about you?" Pete asked, but Snug had already stood up and was on his way to the bar to chat to the girls, who were now pointing and grinning at him. "Yeah. Whatever," he said as he pushed past Frank, who almost tipped his beer. "Watch out!" Frank squeaked. "And you can play Thisbe, Frank," said Pete. Frank was so stunned, he said nothing. Pete took that as a yes and scribbled it down in his notes.

Tom watched Nick texting and then asked, "Have you thought about getting a new phone case?" "What?" "New phone case? I'm selling them at the market at the moment. I've got a few which would be perfect for a bloke like you." Nick blinked and then turned his attention back to Pete. He and Robin were having a discussion about costumes and props. "So, do you have lots of creative ideas?" Robin asked, "This is so cool." "Well, we have to keep props to a minimum ….," Pete began. "Cool," Robin interrupted, "So people instead of props? People would play the objects like moonlight and the wall. Wow! That's revolutionary, Pete!" "Ummm, yeah, I guess so …" "I could be the moonlight and stand on a chair and point a spotlight or something and Tom could be …" Robin considered Tom for a moment. "The wall!" Robin said, getting really excited now. Everyone looked at Tom who was still examining Nick's phone. Noticing all eyes were on him, he put Nick's phone down. At that moment there was a loud shout from the bar and everyone turned to see what had happened.

A rather large man had arrived and was not pleased to find Snug flirting with his girlfriend and his sister. Snug grabbed his glass and headed back to the table, briefly looking back at the girls once he had sat down.

"What about costumes? I could sew them at my workshop," Robin said. "That would be great! Maybe you could all discuss what we need," said Pete, looking at his watch and standing up. "So, that's all sorted! I'm sorry, I've got to dash!" "I thought we were going to start rehearsals," said Nick, who couldn't hide his disappointment. "No time today, I'm afraid," said Pete as he drank the rest of his warm beer. "So, when and where do we rehearse? And when is the first gig?" asked Nick. As Pete pulled on his jacket, he said, "Rehearsals every Wednesday at the Village Hall. The first wedding is on the 20th." "20th July? We'll have to get a move on!" laughed Nick and looked around the table at the others. "No. 20th June." "20TH JUNE?! That's in 2 weeks!" squeaked Frank, who had finally got over the shock of being cast as Thisbe and found his voice again. "Yep. See you Wednesday!" and with that Pete was gone.

Robin immediately began talking about all the cool ideas he had for costumes while the other members of AThENS examined the bottom of their empty beer glasses and asked themselves why they had agreed to this. Except Nick, of course. This was his destiny. He knew it. The beginning of an exciting career as a successful actor. NICK BOTTOM could see his name in lights!

Bottom's Dream

18th June

VOCABULARY

If you **know** a song or poem **off by heart**, then you know all the words.

A **cue** in the theatre is a word or action from another actor which tells you it is your turn to speak.

If you are having a party, you might put out some **nibbles**. These are small things for people to eat.

To stumble means to fall or nearly fall when you are walking. You can also **stumble** over your words.

If you **catch a glimpse of** something, you only see it for a short time.

When we cannot sleep, we often **toss and turn**.

"Nick, you're looking a bit rough!" squeaked Frank as the two men got in the bus to go to work on Thursday morning. "And what have you done to your hair?" "Didn't sleep well," Nick mumbled. "You haven't got cold feet about Saturday, have you?" Nick mumbled something and Frank decided it was probably better to leave him in peace.

Nick didn't usually dream at all. Or at least he never remembered any of his dreams. But that dream last night was something else. They had met for the second rehearsal of the Pyramus and Thisbe play on Wednesday night. The others had been very critical of the way Nick looked and that had upset him a little. Robin said he thought Nick might be a better Pyramus if he had his hair cut before Saturday. Nick had been trying to grow a beard and thought it looked quite fetching. However, Tom suggested he might like to shave it off and had an electric razor going cheap if he was interested.

Apart from that, the rehearsal had gone quite well. Nick knew his part off by heart. Frank kept missing his cues but made a surprisingly attractive Thisbe. Snug's lion was not very enthusiastic but at least he knew his lines! In contrast, Robin was a little too excitable and once fell off his chair and dropped his torch. Tom was still worried the story was too tragic for a wedding. He said he was selling some balloons and party articles down the market. He could bring some along at a reduced price. "Just to cheer everyone up at the end, you know?" Pete was unsure and said he'd have a think about it. He suggested he could bring his accordion along and maybe play a sad piece by some Russian composer at the end. The others weren't convinced but he said he'd bring it along just in case.

At the end of the rehearsal, everyone was a bit weird and kept saying Nick was different to normal. He felt fine, just tired. He went straight to bed when he got home but then he had the most bizarre dream. He dreamt he was in a wood. All the other actors were there practicing. He went up to them but they all screamed when they saw him and ran away. As he was standing on his own, he suddenly saw Jenny Titan in the wood. But she wasn't the shy young girl he knew from work. She was chatty and lively and ... interested in him! In fact, she was all over him. It was weird because some of the other people from work were in the wood, too. And they seemed to be serving Jenny. Even the boss, Mr Mustardseed was fussing around her, bringing her drinks and nibbles.

He tried to remember exactly what had happened. He remembered her kissing him ... but after that ... nothing. He only remembered waking with a start in the morning. He felt ... strange ... but also happy. As he stumbled into the bathroom, he caught a glimpse of himself in the mirror and almost screamed. What had happened to his hair? He must have tossed and turned so much in the night. His long hair was standing on end on each side of his head like long ears. Robin was right. The hair had to go. And so did the beard! He would make a barber's appointment for the evening after work. He looked at himself in the mirror again and remembered a little more of his dream ... and smiled.

Bottom's Big Day

20th June, Midsummer Night

VOCABULARY

A **reception** is a formal party. A **wedding reception** is the celebration after the ceremony.

To chat means to talk about something. **To chatter** is when people talk a lot about things which are not important. You can also use it for the noise that animals make.

If you are embarassed, you turn red or **blush**.

Sometimes if the audience does not like a performance, they may start shouting at the performers. This is called **heckling**.

A **hiccup** (sometimes spelled hiccough) is when you make a repeated noise in your throat which you cannot control. It often comes if you eat or drink too quickly.

*A dead body is called a **corpse**.*
*The **lawn** is a well cared for piece of grass.*

The big day arrived. It was the longest day of the year and Nick woke to find the sun shining. It promised to be a lovely day for the wedding. Nick didn't know the bride and groom but he was pleased they would have a nice sunny day and he was really looking forward to the performance in the evening.

The AThENS group met at 11 o'clock in the Village Hall for a final run-through. Robin arrived with an arm full of costumes and ran around making the last-minute alterations. Frank had learned his lines and Snug had finally got used to the idea of being a lion and was roaring quite convincingly. Pete said he'd make an introduction and explain that Tom was the Wall and Robin the Moonlight in case some of the guests did not have such a good sense of imagination. Everyone thought Nick looked great after his trip to the barber's. Instead of shaving off his beard he had had it trimmed and waxed. They agreed he looked just like the tragic hero Pyramus should. The group left in good spirits and agreed to meet at 6 o'clock at the hotel where the guests were to have the wedding reception.

It really was a beautiful day. It was warm but not too hot and when Nick and the others arrived at the hotel in the evening, Pete ran up to them and told them that, because of the beautiful weather, the bride and groom had asked if it was possible to do an open-air performance. "How cool! How romantic!" Robin said. "Just as well I brought these then," said Tom as he pulled a few sets of fairy lights out of his bag. "My gift to the bride and groom!" he said and then added, "The novelty balloons and the lampions are £5 a bag though."

The group set about decorating the trees and bushes in a small corner of the hotel gardens as the people from the hotel set out some chairs on the grass. Nick felt the scene seemed somehow familiar ... but he knew he'd never been here before. The group went inside to get changed into their costumes. They were chattering and laughing. Frank had a real giggling fit when Nick started doing his vocal exercises so he stopped again and left the room. As he walked out into the corridor, he bumped into someone. "Oh! I'm so sorry! Are you okay?" he said but then he stopped. It was Jenny! And she looked amazing! She always did in Nick's eyes, but this evening ... Wow! "What are you doing here?" he asked, unable to take his eyes off her. "My sister is the bride," she said and blushed. She looked him up and down and then asked, "Are you part of the acting group?" "Yes, I am," said Nick, straightening himself up. "I am the leading man, actually," he said and then wished he hadn't. At that moment the others came out of the room. They were still chattering. "Come on, Pyramus!" Robin said and slapped him on the back. "I'm really looking forward to it," Jenny said. "I'll catch you later!" Nick couldn't say anything and just watched her walk away down the corridor. He turned to join the others so he didn't see her turn around and smile.

Pete was nervous and things got off to a rocky start. The best man and a few of the bridegroom's other friends had already had a few beers too many and started heckling. That made Pete even more nervous. Instead of finding Nick's tragic death moving, everyone started to laugh. It didn't help that Frank got hiccups, so even when he was supposed to be dead, the corpse kept making a hiccupping noise. But Snug and Tom saved the day. Tom got a few of his novelty balloons out and blew them up and tossed them into the crowd. Snug played with some of the children who thought riding on a lion was great fun. Robin did an impromptu light show with his torch before losing his balance and tumbling into the bushes. When Robin had been pulled out again, Pete went to get his accordion but instead of playing a melancholy tune, he started up an Irish folk tune to which Pyramus and Thisbe, who were now alive again, danced a little jig.

"Everyone back inside for the disco!" the best man drunkenly shouted when the guests had finished clapping. Some of the guests walked over to congratulate the actors and said some kind words. The bride and groom shook their hands and said how much they had enjoyed it and told them they could get a drink from the bar.

It wasn't quite the success that Nick had imagined but it had been fun. He also wasn't sure AThENS had a future as a wedding acting group. At least not performing tragic stories from Latin literature. He had to admit that his dream had not come true – it was not the beginning of a career as a successful actor.

After they had finished their drinks, he and the others started tidying up. Tom took down his fairy lights, while the hotel staff took the chairs back inside the hotel. As Nick looked around to make sure they had collected all their things, he felt someone touch his arm. It was Jenny. "That was really good fun," she said. "It was supposed to be a serious, tragic play," Nick said. Jenny thought for a moment but then started to giggle. "I'm sorry but it was more comedy than tragedy!" "I know," said Nick. "I'm never going to be the tragic hero. I'm not Nick Bottom: Hollywood actor. Hero of stage and screen. I'm just Nick Bottom, the chubby guy who works at Weaving Mills". With that Jenny kissed him on the cheek. "You can be my hero if you like," she whispered. His eyes widened and his mouth fell open. "That's not a very flattering look," said Tom as he passed, with his arms full of streamers and burst bits of balloons. "We're going to celebrate … or drown our sorrows at the pub. Are you coming?" Then

Tom looked at Jenny who was still smiling shyly up at Nick and Nick who was staring down at Jenny with his mouth hanging open. "I guess not," Tom said and headed off to the others.

"Come on. I'll smuggle you into the disco! I love a wedding disco, don't you?" Jenny said and taking his hand, she led him across the lawn towards the hotel. Pete, Frank, Snug and Robin were waiting for Tom at the other end of the lawn, grinning at Nick. He raised his hand. "Goodnight unto you all!" he called as he gave a theatrical bow to his friends. Jenny laughed and shook her head. Then she pulled him into the group of people who were dancing and singing along loudly to some 1980s hit.

This was not how he had imagined this midsummer evening ending. Nick looked around at the guests. Some were singing, some were dancing. The bridesmaids were standing at the cake buffet giggling and swaying to the music. The bride and groom were sitting at the table as she tried to feed him wedding cake. He had to admit it was a magical atmosphere. Most magical of all was Jenny who was in the middle of the dancefloor, dancing and beckoning to him to join her. Who needed a life as a famous film star when he could be the hero of his own story with Jenny as his co-star? Maybe his dream had come true after all.

THE MERCHANT
OF VENICE

Shakespeare's original

Why is the play called "The Merchant of Venice"?

The merchant in the title is Antonio who borrows money from the Jewish moneylender Shylock to help his friend Bassanio. In the Middle Ages, Christians could not ask interest when they lent money. This is the reason that moneylenders were often Jewish.

Although Antonio is the character of the play's title, it is probably Shylock who is the most memorable character. In Shakespeare's time, England and the rest of Europe were anti-semitic. Christopher Marlowe also had a tragedy called "The Jew of Malta" which played on the beliefs of the day. Especially when seen from a 21st century perspective, this anti-semitic portrayal of Shylock makes the audience feel uncomfortable. There is, however, a central speech by Shylock which suggests that he only behaves the way he does because of the way he is treated by Christian society:

> I am a Jew. Hath not a Jew eyes?
> Hath not a Jew hands, organs, dimensions, senses, affections, passions?
> Fed with the same food, hurt with the same weapons, [...]
> If you prick us, do we not bleed?
> If you tickle us, do we not laugh?
> If you poison us, do we not die?

What's the original play about?

"The Merchant of Venice" is a typical Shakespeare play with lots of characters and parallel stories. Antonio borrows money from Shylock to help his friend Bassanio who wants to marry Portia. Shylock lends Antonio the money but says that if Antonio cannot repay him, he will take a pound of Antonio's flesh.

Portia's father wants Portia to marry the suitor who picks the casket which contains a portrait of Portia. There are three caskets (or boxes): a gold one, a silver one and a lead one. We see two men choose the wrong caskets before Bassanio arrives with his friend Graziano and chooses the right one. Graziano falls in love with Portia's servant, Nerissa. The women each give their suitor a ring. In the meantime, Shylock's daughter Jessica runs away with a Christian called Lorenzo.

News reaches Venice that Antonio's ships have sunk. This makes it impossible for him to repay Shylock and Shylock takes Antonio to court to make sure that the agreement is kept. When Bassanio hears about what has happened he travels back to Venice. Portia and Nerissa dress up as a lawyer and a clerk and successfully defend Antonio against Shylock. To punish Shylock, he is forced to become a Christian and leave his money to Jessica and Lorenzo when he dies.

Bassanio and Graziano do not recognise the lawyer and his clerk and in thanks, they give them the rings they received from their lovers. When they and Antonio visit Portia and Nerissa later, they have to explain why they gave the rings away. The women forgive them and Antonio hears that his ships have not sunk after all. The couples prepare to marry.

What about this version of the story?

For a modern audience, the play appears not only anti-semitic but also sexist. In today's world, Portia and Nerissa would have no need to dress up as men in order to be accepted as legal professionals. It is also hard to imagine a woman marrying a man just because he chose the right casket and forgiving him so easily if he gives away a precious ring to a stranger.

When I wrote this version of the story, I wanted to make it modern but still keep enough of the story for the reader to recognise Shakespeare's original.

My Shylock is not a Jew but a payday lender. **Payday lenders** offer loans which you can get quickly and easily but with extremely high rates of interest. People who take loans with these lenders are usually people who cannot get a loan from a bank. There are many stories of payday lenders taking money from customers' bank accounts or threatening customers who cannot pay.

Language focus

Finding a partner - now and then

In Shakespeare's plays, young people fall in love and marry within hours. Real life in Elizabethan England was very different to life on Shakespeare's stage.

The richer the people, the more likely it was that a marriage would be arranged by their families. Only fools or poor people married for love. When a woman married, her family paid a dowry which could be money, property or other goods.

In "The Merchant of Venice", we see a number of romantic relationships. Lorenzo and Jessica fall in love and run away together. Jessica's father Shylock sees this as a huge insult.

Portia's father makes plans to arrange her marriage before he dies with his rule about the caskets. Although it is not explicit in the text, it seems that Portia is trying to influence the process. For example, she tries to get Bassanio to spend a few days with her before making a decision.

In the 21st century, in the West, we cannot imagine young people agreeing to an arranged marriage. Most people meet their S.O. ("significant other", their partner) in their daily lives, at school, at work or through friends. However, a study in 2019 found that more than 20% of couples met their partner on a dating app.

Worldwide, 300 million people use a dating app. Tinder is the most often downloaded app in the world. There is also an app called Bumble which was created to give women more control over the dating experience.

If you use a dating app, you upload a **profile** which usually includes a photo and some information about yourself. There were online dating platforms before Tinder, but it was Tinder that made an app for smartphones. Now, if you like someone's profile you **swipe right** and if not, you swipe left.

In the original "The Merchant of Venice", Portia's father was an extremely rich man. In this modern version, he made his money with a technology company. Instead of the men visiting Portia to choose a casket, Portia uses a dating app to find a partner. She is clever and this modern story can allow her to find meaning for her life outside of marriage.

Swipe right

VOCABULARY

*If someone has a **fortune**, they have a lot of money.*

*To be **distracted** by something means that you allow something to take your attention from what you should concentrate on.*

Portia sat in the kitchen, her head resting on her hand. Her tablet computer lay in front of her, showing a photo of a smiling man. She looked bored as she watched Nerissa decorate the cupcakes she had made.

"Has he signed up yet?" asked Nerissa and nodded at the tablet on the table. "No," Portia sighed and swiped the profile of the smiling man to the left.

"What was my father thinking? None of these idiots are really interested in me."

"Why do you think Bassanio hasn't signed up yet?" Nerissa looked at her friend and waited for her answer.

"I guess he still doesn't have the money," Portia said and looked out of the window.

Portia thought about her father and the days before he died. Her father had been the CEO of a globally successful technology company. That company had made him one of the richest men in Italy. One of his most lucrative products was a dating app called Cinder. The name Cinder referred to the story of Cinderella and the advertising line was: "Don't wait for your fairy godmother, take control of your own future, with Cinder!'". A woman could sign up on the website for free and create her own page. Men who wanted to use the website had to pay 500 euro before they could see any profiles. If a man was interested in meeting up, he could then upload his details and wait for an answer. The woman could find out about the men but the men had no way to contact the women until they had agreed. Some women set the men riddles which they had to solve.

Portia hated the website. She thought it had become a game for the women to find a rich partner. But Portia's father insisted that it was a safer platform for women. "The woman is in control!" he said, "It's the perfect dating app for modern feminists!"

When he became ill, he began to worry that Portia would marry someone who was only interested in the family fortune. A friend of Portia's father who was a lawyer had called a number of times to write her father's will.

Balthasar was kind and patient when her father died and explained the conditions of the will. "I know you're angry," he said, "But I really believe your father thought he was protecting you." "Did he think I would throw myself at the first man I meet?" Portia shouted, as the tears streamed down her face. Under the conditions of her father's will, Portia could not get married for the first 18 months after his death. For the first year, she was not allowed to date anyone at all. If she did, she lost all the shares to his company. After a year, she could start dating via Cinder. She had to use it for at least another six months before she could start dating someone who was not registered on Cinder.

He had set up the account for her on Cinder. As well as details about Portia, he added a riddle. If a man got it wrong, he was immediately removed from the page, told not to try to contact Portia and sent a long legal text warning him not to talk to anyone about the riddle.

The riddle was a picture of three boxes. Each box had a description. Underneath the gold box, it said, "If you choose me, you will get what many people want." Underneath the silver one, "If you choose me, you will get what you deserve." Finally, the lead box promised, "If you choose me, you will risk everything." If a man clicked the right box, a picture of Portia would appear and he could go on a date with her if she agreed.

Portia did not know exactly what happened when someone clicked on the box, but she guessed her picture would be in the lead box. A man who chose the lead box was a man who was not distracted by riches. She also guessed that most men would choose either the gold or silver box. The men could log on to her profile but they could only try and solve the riddle if she gave them access. Even if they got it right, Portia did not have to go on a date with them. Her father made sure that she was in control all the time.

She decided to give her father's idea a chance.

A waiting game

After her father's death, her friend, Nerissa had moved in with her. If it had not been for her, Portia would have gone mad. Nerissa was practical and she had a great sense of humour. They had gone to school together and they got on really well. Nerissa loved baking and every day the house was filled with the smell of a new cake recipe she was trying out.

Nerissa had short, dark hair and brown eyes. She almost always wore black and the only piece of jewellery she wore was a pendant with a cupid on it. When Portia first met her, she thought she wore it because she was romantic. Now she knew the opposite was true. Nerissa wore it to remind herself that love was blind. "You can only find true love – if it even exists – by using your head, not your eyes," she always said, tapping her head with her finger.

Portia was clever and had done well at school but did not know what she wanted to do with her life. Her father got her jobs in all the departments in his company but she hated them all. After his death, she left and got a job in the coffee shop where Nerissa worked. She did not need the money but she was glad to have something to keep her busy and it was fun working with Nerissa, even if the boss was quite grumpy.

It was in the coffee shop that she met Bassanio. One day, about nine months after her father's death, he came in with his friend Graziano. Graziano was well-built, loud and confident. Bassanio was tall and slim and very good looking, but unlike Graziano, he was shy and quiet. They had only been in the café for five minutes before Graziano started flirting with Nerissa. Bassanio did not say much, but kept looking at Portia who was busy making coffees for the customers. Whenever she caught him watching her, he smiled shyly and then looked away awkwardly.

Every day, Bassanio came to the café. He leant his bicycle up against the lamppost outside, took off his bicycle helmet and came in. As he waited for his coffee, he chatted nervously to Portia. Slowly she got to know him a little. He had grown up in the poorer part of the city. He had studied business but he was having trouble finding a job. He was working as a courier, delivering parcels on his bicycle while he was job hunting. When they met, he had no idea who Portia was, so she was sure he was not a gold digger. She told him that she had recently lost her father but she did not tell him that her father had been one of the richest men in Italy. He was kind and a good listener.

When he had asked her on a date a few weeks later, she finally told him who she was and that she could only date someone who had registered with Cinder. He looked disappointed but he understood that she wanted to respect her father's wishes. He promised her that he would find the money somehow.

Two months on, she was still waiting for his profile to appear on her account. She had not seen him for weeks and she was worried that he had lost interest. Graziano and Nerissa had been on a few dates and Graziano often came to the café to see her. However, Bass was never with him. He was taking extra shifts to earn money, Graziano said. She hoped that meant that he was trying to save the money to register on Cinder and not that he was avoiding her.

Her profile had been visible for a month now. Every evening, she and Nerissa would sit and look at the profiles of the men who had started logging on to her page. For Nerissa, it was a game. To keep Portia amused, Nerissa started giving the men nicknames.

Scrolling through the profiles one evening, one striking face appeared on Portia's screen. "Oh, I say!" said Nerissa. "He could be a model! Or enter a beauty contest or something! Mr Morocco!" "He is quite good looking," Portia had to admit. The photo showed a black man called Hamza in his mid-twenties. He was very serious in the photo but extremely handsome. His profile said that he was originally from Morocco, that he lived in Venice and owned a few expensive hotels in the city.

"What about it then?" Nerissa looked at her friend. "You could just let him access the riddle and see what happens. You don't have to actually go out with him."

Portia thought for a moment. "I'm not sure," she said. "What have you got to lose? And at least then you can see what your father put in those boxes." Portia looked at the photo again and then swiped right. The girls looked at each other and started to laugh. "Let's see what Mr Morocco chooses then!"

Mr Morocco

VOCABULARY

*The bones in the head are called the **skull** .*

*If you describe what someone says as **harsh**, then you think it is unkind, unfair or unfeeling.*

The next day, in the manager's office of one of the most expensive hotels in Venice, a man was shouting down the phone at one of his employees. He put the phone down noisily and his mobile pinged. Hamza glanced at it. Seeing that there was a notification on his Cinder app, he picked up his mobile and opened the app.

He hardly looked at the clues but immediately clicked on the icon of the gold box, confident that he had made the right decision. The box on the screen dramatically opened and showed a picture of a skull.

A scroll then unrolled with the words:

> Not everything shiny is gold!
> I'm sure that's something you've been told.
> If you'd been wise instead of bold,
> Your chances now would not be cold.

Hamza's face showed no emotion. The phone on his desk rang. He quickly closed the app and answered the phone. Soon he was once again shouting at one of his employees, as if nothing had happened.

Meanwhile, at the girls' flat, Portia's tablet pinged. She was not surprised that he had chosen the wrong box but now at least she could see what her father had written. Nerissa looked over her shoulder, "Oh, that's harsh," she said and pulled a face.

"Never mind," she said breezily. "More important things to do. I need you to tell me which of these cakes is best!" Portia shook her head and followed her friend into the kitchen where they spent the rest of the afternoon comparing chocolate cakes and drinking tea.

Don Juan

VOCABULARY

*A town or village which is close to the sea is **coastal**.*

*If someone's **pride is hurt**, then they are hurt because something has happened which they feel they did not deserve.*

*A **rhyme** is a small poem where the words at the end have the same sound.*

*Someone **cringes** if something happens which makes them feel uncomfortable or embarrassed.*

A week later, there was still no sign of Bassanio logging into the site. "I wonder what's in the silver box," Nerissa said as she and Portia sat together on the patio. Nerissa got up and went into the house. She came back with

Portia's tablet. Portia rolled her eyes. "Let's just have a look," said Nerissa and handed the tablet to Portia.

Portia opened the app and they started scrolling through the new profiles. Before long they came across a profile with more photos than most. Portia clicked on the picture of a Spanish man wearing dark sunglasses.

There really were a lot of photographs. In most of them he was wearing the same dark glasses so Portia could not really tell what he looked like. In one of them, he was driving a convertible along the promenade of a Spanish coastal town with his arm around a pretty girl. In another one, he was leaning against the wall outside a beautiful villa, and in the third, he was shirtless at the wheel of a yacht. One of the photos was a close up and there Portia could see that his hair was starting to go a little grey. That must be why he had sunglasses on in all the photos, she thought. The glasses were hiding his wrinkles.

"Don Juan," Nerissa said as she looked over Portia's shoulder. His profile said that he had made his money selling ice cream. He had started with a stall on the street and now had a café in every town in northern Spain. "Now *that* suddenly makes him *very* attractive!" said Nerissa, laughing and Portia elbowed her playfully. Then she shrugged and swiped right.

Portia imagined this man studying the riddle. She did not like the look of him but she knew his pride would be hurt if he clicked on the wrong box.

In a bar in Barcelona, 'Don Juan's' phone pinged. He opened the Cinder app and smiled. His finger hovered over the gold box but then he clicked on the silver one.

The silver box opened and out came a clown, making faces and laughing. A text box opened and he read:

> I am guessing you feel put down
> Now that you have found this clown.
> When your hair is as silver as this box,
> You will still be an ox.

He was furious. He took a deep breath. He looked up and saw a group of girls at the bar drinking cocktails. One of them was smiling at him and playing with her hair. Who needed this rich heiress anyway? he thought to himself. He got up and ran his fingers through his hair. Then he walked over to the girls, smiling.

Portia and Nerissa saw the rhyme and Portia cringed. "Your dad didn't hold back, did he?" Nerissa said as she read it. Portia was about to answer her when her tablet pinged. She sighed and checked her notifications. Her eyes widened and she opened her mouth. Then she turned to Nerissa and let out a squeal. "He's logged on! He's done it!" Nerissa smiled and the two friends clinked their glasses.

Mr Right?

"That's the second order you've got wrong today," said Nerissa as she brought a cup of coffee back to the counter. "It's a good job the boss is out for a bit." "I just can't concentrate," said Portia. "I don't want to give him access to the riddle before I've got a chance to ...

give him a clue." The bell over the café door rang and Nerissa looked up. "Well, now's your chance," she said and nodded towards the door. There was Graziano and behind him was Bassanio, playing nervously with his helmet.

"You look fine!" whispered Nerissa, as she saw Portia fussing with her dress out of the corner of her eye. The men came over and Graziano gave Nerissa a kiss.

Bassanio was wearing a new pair of jeans, a clean white shirt and a suit jacket. Portia noticed these things and wondered where he had found the money but she was just glad he was there.

Graziano was talking non-stop as usual and Nerissa was laughing at his jokes. Portia looked at Bassanio and quietly asked, "Would you like a coffee?" She was gripping the edge of the counter because her hands were shaking so much.

Suddenly Nerissa interrupted Graziano and said loudly, "It's really warm today, isn't it? My legs are like lead." Nerissa stressed the word "lead" and Portia made a face at her friend. Bassanio and Graziano looked a little confused but Graziano just shrugged and immediately started talking again as if she had not said a word.

A few minutes later, Nerissa turned the discussion to one of the local churches. Local youths had tried to steal the lead from the roof. "Lead is very valuable. Did you know that, Bass?" Bass again looked puzzled. Portia looked embarrassed and widened her eyes at Nerissa, as if to say, "Stop it!" Bassanio watched them and said nothing.

With that, the bell over the door rang again and the café boss came in. Nerissa immediately took a cloth and started wiping down the tables. As he passed, he glared at Graziano and Bassanio. He was a little fed up of these young men coming in and distracting his staff. Graziano took the hint and he and Bassanio left. At the door, Bassanio turned around and gave Portia a little wave and then they were gone.

At the end of their shift, Nerissa and Portia sat down in the backroom of the café and Portia swiped right on Bassanio's profile, giving him access to the riddle.

Meanwhile, Bassanio and Graziano were sitting in a noisy bar in the city looking down at Bass's smartphone. Bass looked at the picture of the boxes and smiled as he remembered Nerissa's clues about how valuable lead was. Without any hesitation, he clicked on the icon of the lead box. The box opened and music started to play. A photo of Portia came out of the box and a text which read:

"You did not choose by sight
But I say that you chose right.
Be happy with the choice you made.
You may now date the beautiful maid!"

Graziano slapped his friend on the back. "Bring on the double dates!" he said, "I'll get us a drink to celebrate." Graziano made his way over to the bar, leaving Bassanio looking down at his mobile.

Short-lived joy

VOCABULARY

To **mumble** means to speak unclearly so that people have trouble understanding.

If you **threaten** someone, you tell them you are going to do something bad or harmful to them.

If you **have history with someone**, it means you have experienced something with them before and it is usually not good.

If someone wants **revenge**, they want to hurt someone who hurt them.

Someone who is **ruthless** is not afraid to hurt other people to get what they want.

The next evening, the two couples celebrated at Portia's house. Bassanio arrived wearing another smart new jacket and shiny new shoes. They were drinking on the patio when Bassanio's phone rang. He looked at the number and frowned. "I'm sorry. I have to take this," he mumbled and walked a few feet away from the others. Portia watched him carefully and could tell something was wrong. Graziano was also watching him nervously and joined him as soon as he had finished talking on the phone. As Portia watched the two men talking, she wondered what it was that worried them so much.

"We have to go and see a friend," Bassanio said when they re-joined the women. "Tonight?" Portia said. Bassanio took a deep breath and began to explain.

"I didn't have the money to register on Cinder. I didn't know what to do." Bassanio hung his head. "I borrowed some money from a good friend, Antonio. He has his own business. What I didn't know is that his business is in trouble. He borrowed the money from a payday lender to give to me. Now the lender wants it back and is threatening to kill him."

"How much does he owe, for goodness' sake?" Portia asked. "Two thousand euro," said Bassanio looking at his feet and his new shoes. "Is that all?" Portia laughed. "Why is he threatening to kill him over two thousand euro?" "He and the lender have history," Graziano said. "The lender is taking him to court. He wants revenge and he's insisting that Antonio keeps the contract. The case is in court tomorrow."

"What on earth did he promise in the contract?" said Nerissa. The two men looked at each other awkwardly. "Antonio said he didn't care if it cost him an arm and a leg. He just wanted to see me happy." The women looked confused, and Nerissa glared at Graziano. "So, what's in the contract? I don't understand." "Two thousand euro for an arm and a leg if he couldn't pay it back," said Graziano quietly.

Portia was horrified. Nerissa thumped Graziano. "Men! Honestly! How stupid can you be?" Graziano opened his mouth to answer her but, looking at Nerissa, thought better of it.

The four talked for hours. ShyLock Payday Lenders were well-known for being ruthless. They were a law unto themselves. They decided Bass and Graziano would go and see Antonio. Portia would give them two thousand euro and they would try and persuade the lender to let them repay it.

Bassanio and Graziano left straightaway, leaving Portia sad and worried and Nerissa seething with anger. As they were saying goodbye, Portia gave Bassanio her father's ring. She had kept it with her ever since he had died. She was afraid of losing Bass again and she wanted to give him something to remind him of her. Nerissa did not have a ring but she did have her pendant. She thought for a moment and then hung it around Graziano's neck before giving him a kiss. And then thumping him again.

The women finished the champagne on their own. Rather, Nerissa finished the champagne and then they went to bed, though neither of them got much sleep. Portia lay awake going through it all in her head and by the morning, she had a plan. She just needed to make a few telephone calls.

When Nerissa came into the kitchen, Portia was on the phone. She was surprised to see Portia up and dressed and she appeared to be making arrangements for a trip. When she finished, she turned to Nerissa, "We're going to Venice for the day!" "What? Where? Why?" Nerissa was not yet fully awake. "We're going to see Bass and Graziano." "I thought we were staying here while they sort out the mess they got their friend into." "They're not going to see us," said Portia. "What? We're going to see them but they're not going to see us? I don't understand!" Nerissa sat down and poured herself a coffee.

"Well, they will see us but they won't recognise us. Come on! Get dressed! I'll explain everything in the car."

Frailty thy name is woman?

VOCABULARY

Someone who is a **big shot** is an important person.

A **mayor** is elected by the people and is the most important official in a town or city.

If you **lean close** to someone, you move your body towards them.

A lawyer who **represents** someone speaks for and acts for someone in court.

To **show mercy** means that you treat someone kindly and sometimes not as they deserve.

If you **pretend** to do something, it means you act in a way that makes others believe you even though it is not true.

*To be **desperate** means that you are in a difficult situation and you are very worried because you do not know what to do.*

*A person who is **determined** does what they have decided to do. They do not let anyone else stop them from doing it.*

*You **presume** something is true, if you believe it is likely although you do not know for sure.*

*If someone says, "**You are a disgrace!**" they are very angry about how you have behaved and think you should be ashamed.*

*To **rush** means to hurry or do something quickly.*

When Portia had told Nerissa her plan, Nerissa thought she had gone mad. How would they get away with it? Surely Bass and Graz would recognise them. The women drove to Balthasar's house. He told Portia exactly what to say and his wife helped Portia into some of her husband's robes. By the time she put the wig on and a thick pair of glasses, even Nerissa did not recognise her friend. Nerissa then dressed up as her clerk. She combed her hair down over her face and put on a suit and tie.

"Are you sure about this?" Nerissa asked her friend for the tenth time that morning but Balthasar answered for her. "Just keep your cool and act like you are a big shot lawyer. It always works for me!" He winked at Portia and she smiled nervously. Balthasar explained that the judge did not really care about law and order. He was planning a second career in politics. Antonio probably could not expect justice unless the judge thought it would improve his chances of becoming the next mayor.

When Nerissa entered the courtroom an hour later, Graziano was shouting and the court guards were trying to get him to be quiet. At the front of the court, Bass was sitting with a man she did not know but guessed must be Antonio. The man looked really scared. Bassanio leaned close to Antonio and put his hand on Antonio's arm. There was another man who she thought must be from ShyLock Payday Lenders. He looked very pleased with himself. Nerissa thought she must be mad to agree to Portia's plan but it was too late now. She walked up to the judge's chair and handed him the note Balthasar had written for her.

She tried to keep her face hidden but Graziano was too busy shouting to notice her anyway. "Order! Order!" the judge said half-heartedly before taking the note from Nerissa and studying it.

Shouting towards Graziano who was still yelling at the back of the court, the judge said, "Sir, if you do not calm down, I will have you removed from my courtroom!" and then to Nerissa, "Very well, bring the lawyer in."

Nerissa hurried out to find Portia who was waiting outside with Balthasar. The lawyer nodded to Portia, "I'll see you later, back at the house." Portia took a deep breath and the two women entered the courtroom. Graziano was sitting at the back of the court between two guards, still angry but no longer shouting. Bass was sitting next to Antonio, looking worried. The loan shark from ShyLock Lenders was grinning and the judge looked like he wished he was in a café, reading the morning newspaper.

Portia approached the judge and spoke briefly with him, careful to keep her voice as low as possible. She then turned to Antonio to explain that she would be taking on his case. While she talked, she was careful not to look at Bass. Antonio said he could not afford it but Portia said she would represent him for free.

Then Portia cleared her throat and addressed the loan shark. "You must show mercy!" she said simply. He stopped grinning, shocked. Then he burst out laughing. "And why would that be? We made a contract. I only want what I've been promised." "Look, be reasonable!" Bass could not help himself. He was on his feet. "I'll pay you back double what Antonio owes you!"

"Not interested. I just want what the contract says I'm owed." The loan shark did not even look at him. "May I see the contract?" Portia said calmly. The loan shark pushed it towards Portia who pretended to study it. "I'll give you three times the amount!" Bassanio was getting desperate. The loan shark shook his head. "I will never take anything but the conditions of the contract. That's my final word."

"The gentleman is right. The contract is clear: he has the right to demand that Antonio pay him an arm and a leg. We can only call on his mercy." Portia fixed the loan shark with her eyes. "Not a chance," he sneered. "Then there is nothing for it. Antonio, you must pay the man." There was a sharp intake of breath all around the courtroom. Even the judge was suddenly paying attention. Antonio held his head in his hands. Bass was beside himself. "Look, Antonio ... everything I have, all this money, even Portia – nothing is as important to me as you!" Portia froze. "Same here!" came a voice from the back. Graziano was on his feet. "I'd rather my girlfriend was dead than see Antonio suffer at the hands of this loan shark!"

The two women exchanged a look. Portia looked heartbroken. Nerissa looked like she was going to kill someone. Portia thought for a moment. She looked around the courtroom. Antonio had broken down and was crying and Bassanio had his arm around Antonio's shoulder. Then she looked down at the robes she was wearing. When she lifted her head, Nerissa noticed that Portia had a different, more determined look in her eyes.

She turned back to the grinning loan shark. "I presume you have worked out how to take an arm and a leg without shedding any blood." The loan shark looked up. He was not laughing anymore. "There is no mention of blood in the contract," Portia said coolly.

Antonio and Bass looked up and stared at Portia. "You can take an arm and a leg, but no blood. And you must make sure that Antonio does not die. The contract does not allow that." And then, looking at the judge out of the corner of her eye, she added, "How can the government allow such things to happen in our beautiful city? I am just glad that such a good judge would never allow it." The judge called Nerissa and told her to bring him the contract so he could study it again.

The loan shark was stunned. As what Portia had said began to sink in, Bass and Antonio started to laugh. They could not believe it. "Okay, I would never have gone ahead with it anyway!" the loan shark stuttered. "No hard feelings! I'll take your offer to pay the loan back with interest and we'll say nothing more about it." Bassanio started to get Portia's money out.

"Wait!" said Portia to Bassanio. "The lender had decided that he would like to keep the conditions of the contract. He cannot now change his mind and ask for money!" "What?" spluttered the loan shark. "You said, 'I will never take anything but the conditions of the contract.' That was your final word. If you do not take those conditions, then the contract is worthless and you give up any right to claim the money."

"Your Honour!" the loan shark appealed to the judge who was now beginning to enjoy his morning in court. "I have studied the contract. I do not know how something like this was ever allowed. What is wrong with the politicians in this city. It's obviously time for political change! I will be looking to introduce new laws which forbid contracts like this. And," he said, shaking the contract at the loan shark, "I will be forbidding companies like yours to trade in this city! You are a disgrace! This case is closed!"

Graziano rushed to the front of the courtroom to celebrate with Antonio and Bass, nearly knocking Nerissa over on the way. As Portia and Nerissa collected up their papers and got ready to leave, Bass came over, carrying the briefcase with Portia's money. Antonio joined him. "How can I ever thank you?" said Antonio. "We would like to offer you the money we would have paid the loan shark," said Bass. At that Nerissa dropped a pile of papers. Portia refused to take the money although the men offered several times. Finally, Portia pointed at her father's ring on Bass's finger and said, "I will not take the money but I will take that ring from you." "This? Oh, that's nothing," he said and stuck his hand in his pocket. Nerissa raised her eyebrows. "I will take no money, but if you want to show your thanks, I will take that ring," Portia repeated.

Graziano, who had just joined them, said, "I'll give you anything of mine instead." "I'll take that lucky pendant," said Nerissa as quick as a flash. When Graziano hesitated, she turned to Portia and said, "They are obviously not that grateful." "No, no," said Graziano, pulling the necklace over his head and handing it to

Nerissa. "It's nothing special," he said and Nerissa's body tensed. "Go on, Bass, give the lawyer the ring," and then quietly he said, "We'll tell them you lost it or something. They'll never know." Bass was uncomfortable but handed over the ring to Portia. The women were not sure how long they could hide their anger, so they thanked the men and hurriedly left the courtroom. Behind them, the men congratulated themselves and made plans to celebrate.

A change of plan

Portia and Nerissa returned to Balthasar's house to give him back the robes and tell him what had happened. Nerissa got changed and left Portia talking to Balthasar.

As they said goodbye to Balthasar and his wife, the lawyer took Portia's hand and said, "If you need anything, you let me know". Portia nodded and Nerissa wondered what the two had talked about.

It was getting dark when Portia and Nerissa got into the car to drive home. They had just pulled away when Portia's phone rang. It was Bassanio. She put the call on speaker phone. "How did it go?" she asked, trying to sound as if she did not know. Nerissa could hear that Bassanio was in a bar and had already had a few drinks too many. Portia rolled her eyes at her. "Well, that's great," she interrupted. "Why don't you and Graz come round tomorrow with the money and you can tell us all about it. Bring Antonio! I'd love to meet him." There was more drunken shouting but Portia just said, "See you tomorrow then!" and finished the conversation.

On the drive back to their house, Nerissa asked her friend what she planned to do now. "Firstly, get the money back!" she said, without taking her eyes off the road. "What are you going to say to Graz?" "I'll be giving him a piece of my mind," Nerissa said angrily. She looked at her friend. Portia seemed like a woman who had found a new purpose. What that purpose was, was still a mystery and it seemed Portia did not want to talk about it just yet. They drove home in silence.

The morning after the night before

VOCABULARY

Grasp *means to reach out and take hold of something but you can also say* **grasp** *to mean 'understand'.*

Slap *is to hit someone with the palm of your hand. To* **punch** *someone is to hit them with your fist.*

The next morning, Nerissa entered the kitchen to find Portia once again dressed early and reading the newspaper in the kitchen. The doorbell rang and the two women exchanged a look. Portia sighed and Nerissa went to answer the door. Portia waited in the kitchen, going over in her head what she was going to say.

When Nerissa opened the door, she saw the three men standing there. Bassanio was holding a bouquet of flowers while Graziano was holding a bottle of champagne. Graziano took a step towards her and Nerissa took a step back. Graziano looked confused, but Bassanio came in behind him. "Where's Portia?" he asked quietly. "In the kitchen," Nerissa said curtly and took the champagne out of Graziano's hand. "Hey, Portia, come and meet Antonio!" Bassanio called as he went into the house to find Portia.

Antonio followed Bassanio into the kitchen. Portia welcomed Antonio, 'It's nice to meet you. I'm so glad you got out of that crazy contract!' She turned to see Bassanio who was standing a little awkwardly, unsure how to greet her. He offered her the flowers and then the money she had lent him. At that moment, they heard shouting from the hallway. "It wasn't anything special!" Graziano was shouting. "It was special to me!" Nerissa shouted back at him.

Nerissa was still shouting when Graziano came into the kitchen. 'Tell her why I gave away her stupid pendant, Bass!" Portia raised an eyebrow and looked at Bassanio's hand where her father's ring was obviously missing. Bassanio began to explain about the lawyer and his assistant and how they helped win Antonio's case and both Portia and Nerissa listened with their arms folded. "You should have been there. The lawyer was so clever," he said, "You'd understand if you'd been there." When he finished, the two women looked at each other and at the same time they each pulled out the chains which had been hidden under their t-shirts. Bassanio and Graziano gasped. Nerissa was wearing her cupid pendant and Portia had her father's ring on a chain around her neck.

"Didn't you think the lawyer was a little familiar?" Portia said. Bassanio was trying to make sense of the situation but failing. Slowly he started to understand. "You? You were the lawyer? But he was … a 'he'! I don't get it." "I'd rather my girlfriend were dead," Nerissa said, staring at Graziano who was still too hungover from the night before to grasp what was going on.

Antonio was completely lost but it had been a long night and he had also had a lot of alcohol so he gave up and sat down on a chair in the corner.

Bassanio and Portia went into the garden and spent a good half an hour talking. "I do care for you, you know," he said quietly. "Can we still be friends?" Portia smiled a sad smile. "I'd like that. But maybe this will give you a chance to think about what you want from life, too." They looked through the window at the other three in the kitchen. She could see Antonio slumped in the chair. Nerissa was busy kneading some dough. The way she was punching it, Portia knew she was still extremely annoyed. She watched as Graziano moved a little closer to Nerissa. "Don't even think about it!" Nerissa hissed at him raising a finger covered in flour and dough. Graziano

SARAH CURTIUS

took a step backwards and sat down heavily on the chair
next to Antonio.

Blind cupid

Two years later ...

VOCABULARY

*If a business **expands**, it is taking action to grow.*

———— *ele* ————

As Portia entered Nerissa's new café, she thought about all that had happened in the two years since the court case. Portia stood and waited while Nerissa served the stream of customers.

While she waited, Portia looked up at the sign on the wall of Nerissa's café "Cupid's Cakes". Underneath the name was a picture of a chubby, blindfolded Cupid with a bow in one hand and a cake in the other.

"You're doing well," Portia said, looking around at the small café, full of chatting customers. "Opening this place was the best decision I ever made. No more grumpy bosses," Nerissa said, wiping her hands on a towel. "What about you? A year into a law degree. Any regrets? Would you rather be an unhappily married woman?" Portia shook her head, "No regrets. It's hard work but I'm still enjoying it. I do hope I'll be happily married one day. Just not until I'm qualified."

Nerissa looked up and saw Bassanio and Graziano talking outside. Graziano caught Nerissa's eye and waved and smiled. Seeing her scowl, his face fell and he looked away. He and Bassanio exchanged a few words and then he slapped his friend on the back and walked off. "You're still in touch with him then," said Nerissa nodding towards the door. "Just friends. He's going on a business trip with Antonio for a few weeks and wanted to meet before they leave," said Portia, watching Bassanio straighten his jacket before coming into the café. Nerissa rolled her eyes. "Go and sit down," she said. "I'll bring you some coffees."

Nerissa watched Bassanio and Portia as she prepared their drinks. After the court case, Antonio's business had recovered and he took on Bassanio as a partner in the company. It seemed to be something Bass was good at and the company was expanding into other countries. Bassanio had changed in the last two years. No more torn jeans and scruffy t-shirts. He was smartly dressed and had grown in confidence. A number of the women in the café shot Portia a jealous look as he hugged her and sat down.

What were his feelings for her now? Nerissa could not tell. What she did know was that Portia was a different woman. While Portia had been in love with Bass, she had been blind like cupid. Now she could see clearly and she knew what she wanted from life.

Portia could tell that Bassanio had something to get off his chest. When Nerissa took their coffees over, Bassanio fell silent and looked awkward. Nerissa put the cup down in front of Bassanio. She looked at her friend and just raised her eyebrows at Portia, shrugged and went back to the customers waiting at the counter.

Bassanio waited for Nerissa to walk away before taking a deep breath. "Antonio … he's not just my business partner …" he said. "I know," Portia said simply and smiled. He looked at her, amazed. "How? When? What?" "I think I realised before you did, Bass." Bassanio's shoulders relaxed and he was able to tell her exactly how he felt now that Antonio and he were in a relationship. The two chatted for over an hour until Antonio came in to pick Bassanio up. Bass and Portia hugged as he said goodbye, both glad not to be romantic partners but happy to be friends.

Nerissa came over to join Portia. She was carrying two plates of chocolate cake and fresh coffee. She pulled off her apron and sat down for a short break. "So ... love really is blind, huh? Nobody saw that coming."

Portia put a fork full of Nerissa's award-winning chocolate cake into her mouth and looked around the café at the many couples, friends and families. She swallowed and turned to Nerissa, "You know the "love is blind" thing is from a Shakespeare play? He wrote a lot about love." "I think the guy who drew Snoopy really understood what love is," answered Nerissa. Portia thought for a moment. "Charles M. Schultz?" "That's the guy." "Why? What did he say?" Putting a piece of chocolate cake on her fork, Nerissa looked at Portia and smiled. "Love is all you need. But a little chocolate now and then doesn't hurt."

TWELFTH
NIGHT

Shakespeare's orginal

Why is the play called "Twelfth Night"?

Twelfth Night is the twelfth and last day of Christmas. Nowadays, it is the day on which people take down their Christmas decorations. In Shakespeare's day, it was a night for feasting and drinking. Men dressed as women and vice versa. Servants pretended to be lords and ladies. On the morning of 6th January, order was restored but the night before was wild. We see these role reversals in the play when Viola dresses as a boy and Malvolio, Olivia's servant dresses and behaves like the lord. We also see some wild partying with Sir Toby Belch and his friends. Like the Puritans of the time, Malvolio in the play did not approve of the drinking and feasting.

The first public performance of Shakespeare's play was recorded on 2nd February 1602. However, some people believe that the play was written and performed for Queen Elizabeth I on 6 January.

What's the original play about?

At the beginning of the play, we see Duke Orsino who is in love with Olivia who is not in love with him. Soon Orsino employs a "boy" called Cesario and sends him to woo Olivia. He does not realise that Cesario is actually a young woman called Viola who was shipwrecked along with her twin brother Sebastian. Viola believes Sebastian is dead although he did, in fact, survive.

Olivia is still mourning the death of her father. Her uncle Sir Toby Belch is staying with her. He and his friends like to drink and party and so make an enemy of Olivia's steward, Malvolio. They decide to trick Malvolio into believing that Olivia is in love with him.

In the meantime, Viola visits Olivia, dressed as Cesario, and Olivia falls in love with her. Later, Olivia sends her fool Feste to find Cesario but Feste finds Sebastian instead. Olivia finds Sebastian fighting with one of Toby's friends and takes him back to her house. They soon go off to get married.

Olivia later visits Orsino and wants Cesario to go home with her, calling him "husband". Orsino is angry because he believes Cesario has deceived him but then Sebastian enters and the twins are re-united. Cesario reveals that she is Viola and she and Orsino marry.

What about this version of the story?
When I was thinking about Viola and Sebastian being washed up on a beach, I immediately thought of the photographs we have all seen in the past years of migrants making dangerous journeys in small boats. In this story, I try to imagine how the story could play out with asylum seekers in Dover in the south of England.

Language focus

Shakespeare hints

The stories in this book are based on figures from Shakespeare's plays. However, there are also some Shakespeare quotes hidden in the stories, too. Here are some of them along with other quotes and proverbs.

In the story based on "A Midsummer Night's Dream", the acting group is called AThENS because the original play is set in Athens, Greece.

At the end of the play at the wedding reception, the actors perform a jig. This is what happened in the performances in Shakespeare's times. At the end of the plays, even after tragedies, the actors would perform a little dance.

In my version of "The Merchant of Venice", Portia and Nerissa discuss a Shakespeare quote about love being blind. The actual lines are from "A Midsummer Night's Dream" where Helena says:

> Love looks not with the eyes but with the mind;
> And therefore is winged Cupid painted blind.

In my story, Nerissa wears a pendant with cupid on it and at the end of the story it is also the name of her café.

One of the chapter headings of this story is a very famous quote from "Hamlet":

> Frailty, thy name is woman!

Hamlet says that to his mother because she marries his uncle soon after the death of Hamlet's father. He is disappointed because he thinks she is weak. Of all Shakespeare's plays, "Hamlet" is the one with the most memorable quotes. "To be or not to be ...", for example, is from "Hamlet".

In Shakespeare's "The Merchant of Venice", Shylock asks for a pound of flesh. In my version, I have used an idiom instead. If something costs **an arm and a leg** it means it is very expensive. In the story, Shylock takes it literally.

Finally, in "Twelfth Night", as the characters watch the rain at the end, Viola quotes a song from the original play. Olivia's fool, Feste sings a song which has the lines:

> When that I was and a little tiny boy,
> With hey, ho, the wind and the rain,
> A foolish thing was but a toy,
> For the rain it raineth every day.

The title for the chapter for the Christmas celebration is from a popular Christmas carol:

> Deck the hall with boughs of holly,
> Fa, la, la, la, la, la, la, la, la!
> 'Tis the season to be jolly,
> Fa, la, la, la, la, la, la, la, la!
> Fill the meadcup, drain the barrel,
> Fa, la, la, la, la, la, la, la!

The original words have no religious references and talk about being jolly, drinking and partying. It fits well with the Twelfth Night celebrations of Shakespeare's day.

Shakespeare is probably the most quoted writer of all time. What famous quotes do you know?

Once upon a time, on a rainy evening in December

December 1

VOCABULARY

To **plead** is to ask for something in a very emotional way because you really want it.

The elected government of a town, city or county is called a **council**. The officials who make up the local government are called **councillors**.

A rubber boat is called a **dinghy** and if you travel in one you should wear a **life vest** which you put over your head and tie around your body, to stop you from drowning.

*If you give or **shoot someone a dirty look**, you look at them in a way that shows you are angry with them.*

*If you **scan** something, it means you look at it very carefully, usually because you are looking for something.*

"Have a heart!" Olivia pleaded. "These people wash up on our beaches and they are hungry, exhausted and afraid. They have nothing except what they're wearing. Men, women, children. The youngest last week was just eight weeks old! We have a duty to care for them." "And who's going to pay?" asked an old man.

Orsino had seen the report on council spending in the last twelve months. Everyone wanted money and there was just not enough of it. So much of the area was run down and needed investment. Local schools were asking for money. People wanted a better bus service but did not want to pay any more for it. Everyone was angry about the long queues of trucks on the motorway and through the town because of Brexit. Why wasn't the council doing something about that? The wish list was long and they just did not have the finances for all these things. And then there were the "migrants". The never-ending stream of people arriving on the Kent coast.

"They're not migrants," Olivia explained. "Migrants are people who come because they can. They usually come for work. Refugees are those who have been given refugee status and have the right to remain. These people are …" "Illegal immigrants!" someone shouted and then everyone was shouting again. Orsino sighed and held up his hands, trying to calm everyone down.

Some local people were fed up of all the dinghies and life vests left on the beach. One woman said clothes had been stolen from her washing line and she believed migrants must have done it. As well as Olivia, there were a number of people there from the various organisations who helped the asylum seekers They were shouting about the tragic stories of the people they were trying to help. Orsino was tired. He had heard it all before. He stood up and finally quietened the crowd. Then he asked Olivia to finish what she was saying. "These people are seeking asylum. They have left their countries because their lives are in danger and under the Refugee Convention of 1951, they have a legal right to ask for refuge in another country."

Orsino admired Olivia for her passion and, of course, he was still in love with her. He remembered the first time he had seen her at school. It was love at first sight. But she was lively and interesting while he was shy and boring and was usually reading a book. After school, she had gone to Manchester to study Politics, while Orsino had got a job in Dover. He was a councillor there now.

Olivia moved back a year ago to look after her father who was ill. He died six months later and now Olivia worked for the local newspaper and spent all her free time helping out at the refugee centre. Orsino had tried to ask her out a few times when she got back but she had always said she had to look after her father. He had not liked to ask since her father had passed away.

"Councillor?" Janice, his secretary who was sitting next to Orsino nudged him and tore him away from his memories. The people were still shouting and Olivia was still looking at him with an annoyed look on her face. Orsino got to his feet. "I thank you all for coming along this evening. We have heard all you have to say and we will give it some thought over the Christmas break. We wish you all a happy Christmas and we will see you at the next neighbourhood meeting in January."

The people got up and started putting their jackets on. Most of them were still complaining to the people they agreed with and shooting dirty looks at the people they did not agree with. Orsino was frustrated. People did not listen to each other anymore. They only talked to the people who thought like they did. He collected his papers and thanked Janice, wishing her and her family a lovely Christmas. "You do realise this is the most dangerous time of year for these people?" an annoyed voice said. He looked up to see Olivia. "The mild weather means they are still attempting the crossing, but it's so dangerous. When they arrive, they are wet and frozen to the bone.

We need some kind of help in place when they reach the beaches." "I understand …," Orsino started to say. "Do you?" Olivia was always calm and professional in the meetings but he knew how strongly she felt about this and she was angry. "I'll try my best to talk to the council in the new year …" Olivia scowled, then sighed. "Have a nice Christmas," she said and turned to leave. Once again, he had missed the chance to ask her out. He watched as she picked up her umbrella and left the meeting with her friends.

Meanwhile …

On the same rainy December evening, a small dinghy filled with 20 asylum seekers from four different countries was being tossed around in the middle of the English Channel. It had been a clear day and the famous White Cliffs of Dover had seemed so close but the journey was taking so long. But now it was dark. It had started raining. They were cold and wet. They had no food or water left. A few young children were crying and people were starting to panic. A young Iranian man put his arms around his sister and they tried to keep warm.

After about ten hours, one of the men started talking loudly in broken English on his phone. He was asking for help. Then he spoke to his comrades in a language the others did not understand. Nothing happened for what seemed like an age. Then suddenly someone spotted lights. There were two boats coming towards them. They could hear someone talking through a megaphone but they could not understand what they were saying.

Then everything happened extremely quickly. The man who had phoned for help threw his phone into the sea. People stood up and waved, hoping to get the boat's attention and the dinghy began to take on water. When the boats finally pulled alongside the small dinghy, people started fighting to get off. More water came into the dinghy and people started to panic. The young Iranian woman felt someone push her. She lost her balance. She tried to hold onto her brother but it was too late. She fell into the icy water.

All of a sudden, strong arms pulled her out of the water and on board one of the Border Force ships. They wrapped her in a foil blanket and gave her a bottle of water. She tried to see the dinghy, almost entirely under water by now and scanned the water for her brother but he was not there. She called his name but one of the officials took her and told her to sit with the others. She sat down next to a woman with two small children. The children looked tired and frightened. The little girl was still holding a stuffed toy and stared at the young Iranian woman with wide eyes. She kept looking around for her brother but could not see him. An older woman sat down next to her, looked at her with sad eyes and took her hand. As she patted the younger woman's hand, she said something in a language the Iranian did not understand. Although she could not understand what she had said, she knew the woman's words were kind. They were all cold and exhausted, but at least they were safe. She sat shivering with the others on the deck of the Border Force ship as the sun began to rise and shine on the famous white cliffs.

The Promised Land

VOCABULARY

*A doctor who checks a patient **examines** them.*

*To **beckon** someone means to call them to you without saying anything. Instead you use a gesture, often you use your hand.*

*If you move your hand slowly over an animal or another person, we call that **stroking**.*

When they arrived in Dover, they were taken to a centre where a team of doctors examined each of them, starting with the mothers and children. The young Iranian woman tried to ask whether anyone had seen her brother but she was told that the men had been taken to a different centre. The doctor who examined the new arrivals was kind but tired. She was exhausted by the seemingly endless stream of desperate people who came looking for asylum in this cold, wet country.

After they had been seen by the doctors, they were given food and dry clothes. Then they waited to be interviewed by the British Border Police. A woman beckoned to the young Iranian to follow her. They went into a small room which had two chairs, one on each side of a table. On the table was a monitor and a computer keyboard. The official smiled at the young woman. As she sat down, she pointed to the other chair. "Do you speak English?" The young woman nodded nervously and said, "I have come for asylum." She and her brother knew that it was important to say that in the very first interview on arrival. The official nodded, "Let's start with your name." The young woman hesitated and then said, "Viola." The official studied her for a moment. "Your real name, please." "It is my real name. Saadia Viola. My father was an English Professor. He liked Shakespeare." The official raised her eyebrows and wrote down the names. Then she continued with the other questions.

When she had finished, the official said, "Your English is really good. You won't need any language courses. There's no room in any of the local accommodation centres. You'll have to stay in a 'B and B' until we find you somewhere more permanent." Viola nodded and wondered what a 'B and B' was. But she was cold, tired and hungry and the only thing she could think about was her brother. She asked again how she could find him. The woman sighed. "I told you. I don't know where the people from the other ship went. And anyway, the men won't get a place in the B and B. They'll be taken to the barracks." The word 'barrack' filled Viola with panic. Pictures of soldiers from home flooded her imagination. It was all too much. She broke down and started to cry. The police woman watched her for a moment and then asked, "What's his name? Your brother?" "Sebastian," Viola said between her sobs. The woman stood up. "Come with me. I'll see what I can find out."

They left the tiny room and Viola watched as the woman talked to a colleague with a clipboard. The man shook his head and then the woman came back to Viola. She slowly sat down next to Viola on one of the plastic chairs. "I'm really sorry," she said. "Your brother is not on the list from the other ship." Then she hesitated before she said, "They're not sure whether ..." she paused again and finally looked Viola in the face. "They're not sure whether everyone made it. They think some people may have fallen into the water." Viola felt the panic rising in her chest again. She gasped for air but then she felt someone take her hand. She turned and saw the old woman again. She could not hold back the tears and she sobbed and sobbed while the old woman held her and stroked her long black hair.

The Barracks

December 5

VOCABULARY

When you give money or something else to a charity it is called a **donation**.

If you are cold or afraid, your body might shake. This is called **shivering**.

The colour **navy** *is a dark blue.*

When you are angry, you might close the door loudly behind you. You **slam the door**.

People who help without getting paid are **volunteers**. *To* **volunteer** *is also a verb.*

Olivia took one of the boxes of clothes out of the van and walked over to the barracks. Olivia's organisation collected clothes and brought them for the men. A local supermarket also gave them toothbrushes, toothpaste, soap and deodorant. The £40.85 they got as asylum seekers did not go far and the group tried to help them with any donations they could get.

A group of men were standing outside, trying to get a signal on their mobile phone. Some of them nodded at her as she passed. One of them greeted her by name and she stopped to chat to him. Like all the men here, he had nothing when he arrived except the clothes he was wearing. Olivia asked whether he had had a decision on his application for asylum. He shook his head and shrugged his shoulders. "No news is good news," he said. That was one of the phrases they learned in their English lessons. "I hope so," Olivia answered. "All the best, Mohammed!" she said and carried on to where the other helpers were already sorting through the clothes.

The men were passing the clothes around and talking loudly to each other, but then Olivia spotted a new face. He was standing a bit further away from the others, watching and waiting. Everyone here was sad, angry, or frustrated but Olivia thought this guy looked especially unhappy. He was tall and thin and was wearing a navy pullover and jeans. He was shivering and Sarah, one of the helpers was offering him a jacket. She watched him for a moment and then Halil arrived with another box and asked her if she could get the last one out of the van.

Olivia was trying to hold the box and slam the door of the van at the same time when she heard someone behind her. "Let me help you," the voice said. It was Orsino. He and some people from the council had just arrived to visit the barracks. Orsino took the box from Olivia and Olivia loudly slammed the doors of the van and locked it. "You know it's absolutely disgraceful how these men live here," she started to say. "They're kept like animals. They don't have basic things like food, warm water ..." Orsino sighed. "I know," he said and when she looked at him, she could tell he was also frustrated and unhappy with what he saw. "But you also know that there is not a lot I can do about this. I don't want them to live here like this. It's the Home Office. I've complained a hundred times but they just don't listen." Orsino nodded to the men in greeting as he walked through with the box. Olivia noticed that he greeted them kindly and they all seemed to know him. He came often, it seemed.

He was not a bad man, she thought. He was just doing his job. He put the box down and smiled at the other volunteers. He turned to Olivia, "I have to speak to the new arrivals and try and work out where they're from and what they need. But maybe ..." 'We could go for a drink afterwards,' was what Orsino wanted to say, but he was interrupted by Sarah. "Olivia! Can you give us a hand with the soup?" "Coming!" Olivia called back and left Orsino standing there.

He was still watching her when Janice coughed quietly and handed him a clipboard and a pen. He went inside the barracks and the other council employees called the new arrivals inside. The tall thin man shuffled in with the others. Olivia caught his eye and smiled just as he entered the building. Then he was gone.

The Bookshop

December 12

VOCABULARY

When the government allows people to stay in a country, they are given or **granted asylum**. To grant someone something means to allow them to have what they want.

If you ask for someone to do something in a way that shows how much you want it, you **beg**.

Damp means slightly wet.

If you hit something by accident, we say you **bump into** it.

To **head off** means to go in a certain direction.

Viola had been in the B&B in Dover for two weeks. She now knew that "B&B" stood for "Bed and Breakfast" and was a place British people stayed when they were on holiday. This B&B had beds but no breakfast and she could understand that no British people were coming to this place for their holidays. The B&B had ten small rooms and the whole building desperately needed work done on it. Viola had one of the three rooms on the second floor. The older woman who had been so kind to Viola was next door. Her name was Aisha and she was from Albania. She had come to the UK to join her son and his family but he had not yet been granted asylum and could not take her in. In the third room on their floor was a young woman from Somalia with her little daughter. Viola had heard that her husband had died on the journey through Europe and a cousin had helped them pay the traffickers to get a place on the boat. She spoke no English but she always smiled when she saw Viola. They all shared the bathroom on their floor. The other rooms in the B&B were filled with women from other countries. Some of them had young children. Some of them had already had their asylum interview and were waiting for an answer. Others, like Viola, were still waiting.

They all shared a kitchen and seating area with a few old sofas and chairs downstairs. After they had arrived at the B&B, they had been given a plastic card. An official explained that they could use the card to pay for what they needed. Every week, they could spend exactly £40.85. It was not much. Food was so expensive in this country. Some local women came to the B&B a few times a week and offered English lessons and answered any questions they had. They also offered to help the women get what they needed for the children, find family members who were already in the UK or prepare for the asylum interview. They often brought clothes and food.

Viola was grateful for their kindness but she hated the fact that she needed it. In Iran, they were not rich but they had everything they needed. She did not mind not having money but she missed her books. And she missed her brother.

In Iran, she was studying English. Sebastian, her twin brother, was studying Mechanical Engineering at the same university. Her father had been a professor of English before he retired. He always praised the UK, the way of life and English literature, although he had never visited. As well as their traditional Iranian names, he had given the twins names from a play by Shakespeare. No-one called her Viola in Iran but here in the UK, it was easier for people to say and write and so that was the name she had given when she had arrived.

Viola spent a lot of time thinking about her father. He had been arrested for his political views and the last time they had seen him in prison, he looked very ill. They asked the prison guards to let him see a doctor but he died a week later. After the funeral, Sebastian had been arrested and questioned. He was sent home without charge but it had shaken him. Viola was afraid she would lose him, too. She begged him to leave the country with her and finally he agreed. The trek through Europe had been long and hard. It was often dangerous and they had spent all the money they had but they had always been together.

Now Viola was sitting in a cold, damp room in England alone and it seemed that she had lost him after all. She had asked the helpers who came to the house but there was still no news. She needed some fresh air and, for once, it was not raining. She pulled on the black jacket she had picked out of the box of second-hand clothes and stepped outside. The sun was low in the sky and it was cold. Viola wrapped the scarf around her neck and pulled on her grey hat. She pulled the door closed behind her and set off into the town.

She passed the shops full of flashing Christmas lights. She stopped to look in the window of a bookshop. In the window was a display for a children's book. The bookshop looked so warm and inviting and she decided to step inside. She had always loved books and she soon found the classics that had stood on her father's bookshelves at home. She took an illustrated version of Shakespeare's plays off the shelf and examined it. She thought of her father and tears filled her eyes. She carefully put the book back on the shelf. It cost more than half of the money she had every month. She wondered whether she would ever be able to afford such a book.

As she turned around, she bumped into a man who was holding the hand of a little girl who must have been about six. "I'm so sorry," she said, afraid to look at him. "No worries," he replied kindly. "It's a beautiful edition that," he said and nodded at the Shakespeare book Viola had been holding. "Yes," she said simply. She did not know what else to say. She could see he was looking at her tatty jacket and she felt embarrassed.

"Uncle Orsino," said the little girl, "Can I have a hot chocolate?" "Of course you can!" He looked at Viola again and without really thinking, he added, "Would you like a drink, too?" She lifted her head to look at him and saw that he had kind eyes. He smiled and added, "I mean ... only ... ummm ... if that's okay ...!" Now it was his turn to look embarrassed. He realised it was quite strange to ask a complete stranger to go for a cup of coffee.

At home she would never have gone out with a man alone, especially someone she had never met before. But she was cold and a hot drink sounded wonderful. She looked at the little girl holding her uncle's hand. She was jiggling about and smiling at Viola. "The hot chocolate is the best," she whispered and then added even quieter, "With cream and marshmallows." She giggled and put her hand over her mouth. "Okay. Thank you," Viola said and she followed the man and his niece to the coffeeshop next door.

They ordered their drinks at the till and Viola ordered hot chocolate with cream. Orsino also bought some muffins. He could see the woman was hungry. This strange threesome sat in the coffeeshop until the bored-looking teenager who served them said it was time for him to tidy up and close. The little girl talked and talked and Viola learned a new word from Orsino: chatterbox. The girl's presence meant that it was not awkward to be sitting with this strange man. As she listened to his niece, he studied her face. She looked somehow familiar but he knew they had never met before. He guessed that she had come on one of the migrant crossings. She was beautiful but even when she was laughing with his niece, he could see the sadness in her eyes. He would have liked to know where she was from and how she had ended up here but he did not want to upset her, so he did not ask.

When they went outside, it was dark. He asked where she lived and he could tell that she was embarrassed to say. "We can walk you home," he offered but she shook her head. "Thank you. That was kind of you. People here are kind." "Take care," he said, but she had already turned and was heading off up the hill.

At the beach again

December 15

VOCABULARY

*Using offensive words is called **swearing**.*

*A **gesture** is a movement you make to express something.*

The sun was shining and Olivia decided to get some sandwiches in the supermarket and eat her lunch by the beach. She pulled her scarf a little closer as she turned the corner and a gust of wind reminded her how cold it was despite the winter sunshine.

As she walked down towards the beach, she spotted a figure sitting on the wall. He was wearing a black jacket and a grey woolly hat. She watched as a man with a dog stopped and said something to him. The dogwalker was waving his arms and pointing at the sea. The young man hung his head. As Olivia got close enough to hear what the man was saying, she heard him swear, "Bloody migrants!" He glared at Olivia and then walked off.

Olivia looked at the young man and it was then that she recognised him as the tall man from the barracks. "Sorry about that. Do you mind if I join you?" He looked at her and shrugged and Olivia sat down. She got her lunch out of her bag. "Fancy a sandwich?" The man looked unsure. "Go on. It's just a sandwich!" He gave a nervous laugh and then took one of the sandwiches.

"I saw you at the barracks," Olivia said after a few minutes. The young man looked down. "We brought some food and clothes the other week. I'm Olivia," she offered him her hand. He hesitated but then he took it. "I'm Kareem." "That's a lovely name. What does it mean?" "It means 'noble'," he said. "That's cool. My name just means 'olive tree'." "An olive tree is a noble tree," Kareem said and they both smiled.

"I have a second name, too. I am Sebastian." "That's unusual, isn't it?"

"Yes. My father ..." Olivia watched him. "Tell me. What's your story?". Kareem took a deep breath and then it just spilled out of him. His father's death, his arrest, his sister and the awful journey and the panic on the boat.

"And you're sure your sister didn't make it?" Olivia asked. Kareem shook his head and stared out to sea. "She wanted me to be safe and now I've lost her. And I'll probably be sent back ... or put on a plane to Rwanda. Even if I stay, I am not welcome here." "You have the right to ask for asylum. We can help you prepare for the interview. And don't worry about people like him," Olivia gestured in the direction of the dogwalker. "There are good people here, too."

"What was your sister's name?" Olivia asked. "Saadia. It means 'lucky'." Kareem's eyes filled with tears and he turned his head away from Olivia. "I'm so sorry," she said quietly and he nodded. They sat for a few moments and Olivia looked out to sea. She had heard stories like this so often. Why did Kareem's story touch her so deeply?

After a while, Kareem turned to face her and she could not help but notice again how handsome he was. "Stop it, Olivia!" she said to herself. They had been warned plenty of times about developing feelings for an asylum seeker. It usually got complicated.

"Thank you for lunch. You are a good person," Kareem said and got up to leave. "Wait a minute," Olivia said. "I'd like you to meet more friendly Brits. It will be Christmas soon ..." "We do not celebrate Christmas," Kareem interrupted. "I know," Olivia said. "But if you want to stay, you should get used to some of the culture. The good, the bad and the ugly!" "Which one is Christmas? Good, bad or ugly?" Kareem asked. "All of them usually!" Olivia laughed. "Anyway, we're organising a Christmas celebration on Christmas Day. That's 25th December. It's in the church hall." Olivia started rummaging in her bag and pulled out a crumpled piece of paper. She frowned at it and tried to smooth it before handing it to Kareem. "All the details are on there," she said and added, "There'll be food." "British food?" Kareem asked hesitantly. "Some traditional British food, too but lots of international food. The asylum seekers usually help prepare something traditional from their home countries." Kareem smiled. He carefully folded the piece of paper and put it in his pocket. "Maybe I'll come." "I'll see you there!" Olivia said.

They said an awkward goodbye and Kareem set off to walk back to the barracks as Olivia turned to go back to work.

'Tis the season to be jolly

December 25

VOCABULARY

*If you **dread something**, you do not look forward to it.*
*A **bang** is a sudden loud noise.*
*If family members look alike, someone might say, "**You can't deny the family resemblance**". It means you cannot say that the people do not look like each other.*

Olivia fought with her umbrella as she struggled up the hill in the rain. Typical English Christmas weather! She was going to the Christmas event at the church hall. It was the first Christmas since her father died and she had been dreading it. She did not want to be on her own in the house so she was glad when her Muslim friends Sarah and Halil asked her to help with the event. They had come to the UK as refugees a few years earlier and wanted some local people to take part so that it had more of a British feel. Sarah had told her that someone from the council was coming too and a few people from the church were going to come and sing some Christmas carols after lunch.

Olivia shook her umbrella as she put it down and pushed open the heavy door. She could hear the women talking as they prepared the food and the children playing noisily. Someone had put some Christmas pop songs on in the background. Olivia groaned. She was sick of them. Every shop in town had been playing them since November.

As Olivia went into the main hall, she heard the heavy, wooden door open and close again and out of the corner of her eye she saw someone in a black jacket, a grey hat and a scarf wrapped around their nose and mouth. For a moment she thought it was Kareem. The figure had the same beautiful dark eyes. However, then the figure unwrapped the scarf and took off the hat to reveal a head of beautiful black curly hair. The woman smiled. The smile, too reminded Olivia of Kareem but just as she was going to speak to the woman, someone said, "What this?" A woman in a brightly coloured headscarf held up a red tube and shook it. "What this?" she said again and waved it at Olivia.

Olivia hung her coat up and came over to her. "These are Christmas crackers. Just put one on each place." "What do?" she asked. Olivia explained. "You pull them," she said and mimed pulling the cracker with the woman. "It goes bang!" Olivia mimed surprise at a loud noise. "It has a crown," Olivia mimed putting on a crown. "And a terrible joke and a gift." Olivia did not know how to mime joke and gift so she just grinned. The woman looked at her, said something in Arabic to her friend and started putting them on the table.

The food smelled wonderful. She was a vegetarian so she would not have eaten turkey and she was never a fan of sprouts or Christmas pudding. An oriental Christmas lunch sounded perfect.

Sarah came out of the kitchen and gave her a hug. "It smells amazing," she said. "And I'm starving!" Olivia helped lay the table and carry the food out of the kitchen and an hour later they were sitting down to the best Christmas dinner Olivia could imagine. There were about 40 adults in total. It was mostly families with lots of children and a few single women with children who had come to join their husbands but were still waiting for permission to do so. There was enough food to feed twice as many people.

Olivia kept checking the door but Kareem did not come. In fact, none of the men from the barracks were there. After lunch, the people from the church arrived and set up to play some carols. While they were playing, the wooden door opened and a little girl in bright yellow wellies and a matching raincoat came in. Olivia recognised her. She was Orsino's niece. The little girl was carrying a gift bag and stood shyly looking around the room. She suddenly smiled and ran up to the woman who had come in just after Olivia. She could not hear what they were saying but the woman took the gift and opened it. It looked like a book and the woman hugged the little girl. How did they know each other?

The door opened again and a very wet and dirty Orsino came in. Behind him a group of asylum seekers crowded in and everyone turned around to see what the noise was all about.

"Sorry everyone!" Orsino said. "I didn't want these guys having to walk all the way in the rain. But the council bus broke down and ..." he looked down at his oily clothes. "Well, you're here now!" Halil was on his feet. "And there's still enough food to feed the rest of Dover! Twice!" Halil welcomed the men in but as they started to fill up the places at the tables, one of the women let out a scream. It was the woman who had been speaking to Orsino's niece. Everyone stopped talking and turned to look. There was Kareem, standing like a statue, staring at the woman. Olivia looked from one to the other and then the penny dropped. The woman put the book down and slowly walked over to Kareem. Then she threw her arms around him and sobbed. He was so shocked he could hardly respond but then he held her for what seemed like an age.

Orsino was watching them and looked completely confused. Olivia walked over to join him. "Who? What? Are they ..." he swallowed "Married?" he said. Olivia laughed, "No, silly. They're brother and sister." "But ...," Orsino was really struggling to understand. "His name is Kareem and she's Viola. I didn't think they even came from the same country, let alone the same family." "He's Kareem Sebastian. She must be Saadia. Saadia Viola. Like the twins in the Shakespeare play. And anyway, look at them! You can hardly deny the family resemblance." Orsino looked from one to the other in amazement.

Twelfth Night

January 6

VOCABULARY

Odd can mean strange but it can also mean that things do not match.

*Objects that I own are my **belongings**.*

*On special occasions, we hang up **decorations**. For a birthday, this might be balloons. Especially at Christmas, people hang up a lot of decorations to make their house look special.*

Olivia shook her head again and looked at Orsino. "I don't know how you managed this so quickly." "Where there's a will, there's a way," he replied simply. "Anyway, there have to be some advantages to being a councillor." They were hanging up some curtains which Olivia had bought in a charity shop, while outside the rain was pouring down.

Kareem and Saadia were in the small kitchen, making tea. They could hear them chatting and laughing. The apartment was tiny but it had two rooms, plus a bathroom and a kitchen.

Sebastian's room was the smaller one. The curtains were for the room which would be Viola's bedroom and their living room. There was a small table in the corner and two mismatched chairs. On the table lay an illustrated edition of Shakespeare's works.

Viola came in with the tea and Sebastian was carrying four odd cups from another one of Olivia's charity shop visits. Otherwise, they had two mattresses and some bedding, two black jackets which hung next to the door and the kettle they had just used to boil the water for the tea. That was it.

When Olivia and Orsino had finished hanging up the curtains, Viola went to her small bag of belongings and pulled out a Christmas cracker. "I want to hang this up, too," she said and held it up to Orsino. "But today is January 6th. We take the Christmas decorations down today, not hang them up."

"We have never celebrated Christmas before but now we will celebrate it every day," she said. "You mean, every year," said Orsino. "No. Every day. Every day I will remember how we found each other." She hugged her brother and he kissed the top of her head.

Olivia stood looking out of the window. From there they could see the sea and the ferries leaving the docks. "Will this rain never stop?" said Olivia. Sebastian joined her. "In Iran, rain is seen as a sign of blessing." Olivia rolled her eyes, "Then we must be very blessed!"

"We are," said Viola quietly and looked at Orsino. "Hey, ho, the wind and the rain," He smiled at her and lifted his tea cup as if in a toast. "The rain it raineth every day."

Looking for more?

Visit my blog for an extra chapter about Shakespeare and migration in the 16th century.

https://sarahcurtiusbooks.wordpress.com/shakespeare-and-migration/

About the author

Sarah Curtius is an English teacher who lives near Hanover in Germany. She studied German and English in the UK and Germany and in 2019, she completed her MA in Applied Linguistics and TESOL (Teaching English to Speakers of Other Languages).

When she is not encouraging people to learn English, she loves to paint, sew and do any kind of handicraft. She is proud of her homeland of Wales which is the most beautiful place on earth!

Also by Sarah Curtius

Who are you calling old?

Who are you calling old?

How old is 'old'?
Do *you* feel old?
What happens to us as we get older?
Read about some inspiring people and find out about what happens in our brain as we age and why learning new skills is still possible.

This book is for English learners at CEFR Level B1.
ISBN: 978-3-7543-3070-8
or as an E-book EAN: 783754364185

Order the book here

https://www.bod.de/buchshop/who-are-you-calling-o ldo-sarah-curtius-9783754330708

Coming soon

Wales

A book about Wales, a land rich with history, myths and legends, written for English learners (CEFR B1).

What languages do people speak in Wales?

Who was the first Prince of Wales?

What is the position of Wales in the United Kingdom?

And find out about famous Welsh people you did not realise were Welsh!

Coming 2023

The History Series

Books about British history for English learners (CEFR B1).

As well as the lives of well-known personalities, find out what was happening in science and culture, what every day life was like and read about a scandal or two.

The first book in the series will look at the times of the

Tudor Kings.

Who are the Tudors?

Who was the first woman to publish a book?

Who invented the first watch?

For more information

Find out more about my books, at https:// sarahcurtiusbooks.wordpress.com/

If you are a teacher, you can download some **free** lesson materials https://payhip.com/SarahCurtius

Or visit my blog: https:// nevertoolatelanguage.wordpress.com/

Acknowledgments

Images

Thank you, Iona and Christoph, for your patient proof-reading, encouragement and helpful criticism.

Photo credits
   Cover: Adobe, Stefanina
   page 1: Pixabay, WikiImages
   pages 5, 37, 83: Adobe, Angela